This book belongs to:

....

For my grandchildren—Talulla, Ronin, and Mia—
and for all the children who explore this changing world.

A note about mindfulness

I remember, decades ago, walking down the street with my three-year-old daughter, Vanessa, and learning from her how to be more fully aware of my surroundings. "What's that sound?" she asked. I hadn't noticed a thing because I was so busy with my internal dialogue—thinking about work, worrying about next month's resources—as well as watching for her safety. But when I brought myself more fully present I heard the sound she'd asked me about—a distant wail. "That was a siren," I told her. "The sound a fire truck makes when it's off to help people and the driver wants other cars to give it room." "What's that smell?" she asked. I hadn't noticed, but lilacs were just coming out. "That's the aroma of the lilac bush as it calls to the bees to visit." And as I truly smelled that lilac, I let go of my internal dialogue and became more present to my daughter. We had a lovely, relaxed moment, bonding and learning together, and it became a memory I have cherished all my life.

Children are naturally mindful—aware, attentive, perceptive, and in the present moment—and, as parents and carers, we can help them value these wonderful abilities and keep them available as a resource. The calming practice of mindfulness has been proven to help people lighten their mood, handle difficult emotions, and step out of their anxieties to make better decisions in the present. Not least, through practicing mindfulness we also hear the gentle whisper of our intuition and feel the quiet spark of spirit underneath.

So come walk with Talulla Bear as she explores the world with fresh eyes and learns to be in the moment. Help your little one, and yourself in the process—notice what you notice, become aware of the wisdom of your senses, and be safe and fully present in this unique place on earth, this precious moment in time.

Heather Roan Robbins

TALULLA BEAR
GOES EXPLORING

A Mindful Tale of Discovery

HEATHER ROAN ROBBINS

Illustrations by Sarah Perkins

CICO kidz

Let's go exploring, Talulla Bear.
Exploring?
Yes little one, we've been living in our natural
world of ice and ocean all winter long, but it
is summer now and the ice is melting.

Let's travel and see what the world has to offer.

It's time for us to go on shore and visit

the land of trees and birds.

I've never seen land like this.

Yes, little bear, this land is new to you.

I'm scared.

It's easy to be scared when everything is new,

but I'm here with you.

Together we will find beautiful things

and learn how to walk in new places.

You have the ability to explore safely, my bear cub;

it is all within you.

You know how to breathe,
how to smell the air around you,
how to see, how to hear the sounds,
and feel the ground beneath you.
Simply be aware, my sweet Talulla.
That is all you need to begin.

First, let's take a few deep, slow breaths.

This helps us relax so we can fully enjoy all

this land has to offer.

Raise your nose up and smell the fresh air.

Let it slowly fill you—from your belly, all the

way up, and then gently let it out.

Make room for your next breath.

Breathe in again.

What can you smell?

The air smells different than it did in our winter home,

so many different smells.

There's a green smell from these plants, and a dark,
earthy smell beneath them.
And my nose notices something new,
a pretty and colorful smell.
What is it?

Look on top of that hill. What do you see?
I see bright colors, that lovely smell is coming
from the colors.

Yes, my sweet bear, those plants have flowers,
Can you see the pink, yellow, and purple flowers?
Each one has a different smell,
it's their call to the bees.
Let's go explore.

Listen, what do you hear?

Buzzzzzz

It's the sound of a happy busy bee, a furry, flying bug

buzzing between the flowers.

Do you think the bee wants to play with us?

No, he sounds busy, and he is moving away.

Wise little one!

You're right, he might sting our noses if we poke him.

You have good instincts!

Just by listening and watching, you sensed

he likes to be left alone, you stayed safe.

But we can share the beautiful

flowers with him.

I wonder where his next adventure will take him.

Now, let's walk where a river meets the sea.

What do you feel beneath your feet?

It doesn't feel hard, like ice, or powdery, like snow.

It's all soft and squishy between my toes.

Yes, the sunlight warms the ground,

water seeps in and mixes with the earth,

and together they make mud.

It's a little slippery here, I might fall.

A little mud can be fun, but

walk gently little one.

Let's stop and breathe together again.

Let your breath fill your chest and belly all the way up,

and then gently let it all the way out.

Breathe in and out again, slow and full.

Well done, Talulla Bear. You are so good at breathing!

Do you feel steadier now,

ready to step easily and securely?

Yes, I think I'm ready.

Walk with your weight right over your foot,

like you learned to do on slippery ice.

But this time enjoy the squishy mud beneath your feet.

Make it a game.

When we are calm and aware

we can safely play in the mud and

slide around, just like those slippery seals.

They look like they're having fun!

All this exploring has made me hungry.

Let me show you a sweet and wonderful treat.

What is that?

A berry! Over there on a bush, see the purple blueberries.

Here, eat one. It's tart and fruity.

Hold it in your mouth and let the taste

run all over your tongue.

Does it taste like it looks?

(Giggle) It tastes purple!

It's small but so tasty.

Shhhh, listen. Can you hear a shuffle and a snuffle,
can you feel a thump of big feet on the ground?
It's our cousins, the big brown bears coming to
feast on the berries with us.
Are there enough?
Yes, don't worry, sweet Talulla, there are plenty
of berries to go around.

Are those baby bears like me?

Yes.

I'm scared! I haven't met other bears before.

They may be scared too.

What do we do if we're scared?

Let's do what we practiced...

Let's smell the air around us. What can you smell?

I smell the sea, berries, earth, flowers, and bears nearby.

Listen to the sounds. What can you hear, Talulla Bear?

I hear the wind, the waves, the sound of bees,

birds flying, pushing through the air.

And I hear the shuffling of the bears.

And what can you feel, my sweet Talulla?

I feel the solid ground beneath us, I feel you next to me,

I feel the wind in my fur, I feel excited!

And ready to meet our cousins?

Yes, ready!

Hello! My name is Ronin.

I'm Talulla. Do you like berries?

We can find them by their wonderful smell.

Let me show you.

Yum!

What do they taste like to you?

Like summertime.

Sunny, silly, sweet, tart, and delicious.

And purple!

Let's go play!

We can climb a tree and ask each branch

if it is ready to hold us.

We can see far away!

What an adventure.

Listen, the bees have gone to sleep,

the wind is softer, it is quiet now.

We are full and tired.

It's time to return home, sweet Talulla, back toward the ice.

Bye, bye my lovely friend, Ronin. It was such fun.

Let's meet again soon.

I hear feet stamping and moving.
Look! Families of reindeer.
Let's not scare them, let's be quiet and watch.
Aww, watching them makes my heart
feel warm and happy.

Oh—what a wonderful day.

It's so good to be back in our cool home.

Each animal needs its home,

For us polar bears, ice is best, it is our nest.

I feel happy and relaxed,

and proud of myself.

Ready to explore again tomorrow.

Published in 2017 by CICO Books
An imprint of Ryland Peters & Small Ltd
20–21 Jockey's Fields London WC1R 4BW
341 E 116th St New York, NY 10029

www.rylandpeters.com

10 9 8 7 6 5 4 3 2 1

Text © Heather Roan Robbins 2017
Design and illustrations © CICO Books 2017

A CIP catalog record for this book is available from
the Library of Congress and the British Library.

ISBN: 978-1-78249-471-3

Printed in China

Designer: Emily Breen
In-house editor: Dawn Bates
Art director: Sally Powell
Head of production: Patricia Harrington
Publishing manager: Penny Craig
Publisher: Cindy Richards

For parents Polar bears are adorable, and they are on the front lines of climate change. With less and less polar ice available, they are spending more time on solid ground, a place they always visited, but not a place that sustains their diet. For more information, and for ways to help, see www.polarbearsinternational.org

Acknowledgments This work came from observing young ones and brainstorming with Samantha Moe, M.A. certified parent coach, www.mad2glad.com—thank you. I am grateful for my wonderful illustrator Sarah Perkins who brings to life the stories I see in my heart. I want to thank my family and my animals for taking me out on frequent exploratory journeys—you can make a simple walk around the block a delightful adventure. Thank you to my team at CICO books for making all this possible.

PICTURE CREDITS

Shutterstock: front cover: Sergey Uryadnikov; Eric Isselee • back cover: Shutterstock: Lamberto; Pan_Da • pp.4–5: Keith Levit; Christopher Wood • pp.6–7: Edwin Butler • pp.8–9: Oksana Ariskina; Greeneyesgirl 1967 • pp.12–13: Eric Isselee; Chbaum; Ivaschenko Roman; Kzww • pp.14–15: Igor Kovalchuk; Sergey Uryadnikov • pp.16–17: Bildagentur Zooner Gmbh; Kavel Cerny; Nikishina E • pp.18–19: Lamberrto; Chbaum; Dan Bach Kristensen; Troutnut • pp.20–21: Ondre J Chvatal; David Rasmus • pp.22–23: Attila Jandi; Voronina Natalia; Standret; David Rasmus; Outdoorsman • pp.24–25: Roman Mikhailiuk; Andamanec; ET1972; Katerina Romanova; Jamen Percy • pp.26–27: Sergey Uryadnikov; Tomas Kulaja; Iakov Filimonov; Olga_i • p28–29: Sergey Krasnoshchokov; Pim Leijen; Michal Knitl; Iakov Filimonov; Lamberrto • p30–31: Lamberrto; Andreanita